THE RED BOOK

by **Barbara Lehman**

Houghton Mifflin Company
Boston 2004

For My Father

www.houghtonmifflinbooks.com

The illustrations are watercolor, gouache, and ink.

ISBN-13: 978-0-618-42858-8
ISBN-10: 0-618-42858-5

Library of Congress Cataloging-in-Publication Data is on file.

Printed in Singapore
TWP 10 9 8 7 6 5 4 3 2 1

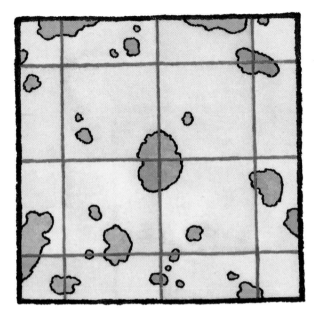